The Kiwi that was Scared of the Dark

Bob Darroch

The little kiwi looked out from the entrance of the burrow.
For the first time, he saw the outside world.
But he didn't like it much — it was dark!

"C'mon," said his mother. "Let's go for a walk."

He followed close behind her, looking fearfully
from one dark side to the other.

From the blackness came scratching noises. And clicks. And rustling.
"What was that?" he whispered loudly to his mother.

"Don't be scared," she said. "It's just insects having their breakfast. See …?"
The little kiwi looked and saw that the insects were small and
too busy eating to take much notice of them.
"Hello," one of them said through a mouthful of leaf.
"Oh — hello," Kiwi replied, not quite as frightened as he had been.

But suddenly fear came back.
A chorus of rattly, croaky noises came from a swampy area nearby.
Then something small leapt out of the darkness and landed close by.
"What was that?" the little kiwi cried.

"That's a frog," said Mother Kiwi. The frog hopped closer.
"Hello," he croaked. "I haven't seen you before. I hope you like it here."
The little kiwi said, "Hello … thank you …", but before he could say any
more the frog had leapt back into the wet place. Perhaps it was just as well
that the frog didn't wait for an answer because the little kiwi still didn't know
if he liked it here. He didn't like the dark.

In fact he was scared of it — especially when an eerie "hoot, hoot"
noise echoed through the trees.

"It's just a morepork," assured Mother Kiwi.
"See, up there in the tree — with a little one your age."
"Hello," everyone called out together.
"When I'm a bit bigger," the little morepork called out, "I'll come and play."
"That'll be good," replied the little kiwi, although he was a bit worried about
playing with someone who made a scary noise like the morepork did.

But a worse noise followed.
A deep, booming noise shook the leaves and the ground.
"What was that?" wailed the little one.
"That's old kakapo. Come, and we'll see him," Mother Kiwi
said as she led the way.
The Little Kiwi didn't want to go near that noise, but he didn't want to be left
behind in the dark either, so he followed close behind.

"Hello," said a small, round shape that came out from a clump of ferns.
"Sorry about the noise. My dad likes to kick up a din every now and then.
I'll go and tell him to tone it down a bit. See you later …", and he scurried off.
Kiwi was relieved that the little kakapo was friendly.
He came from a noisy family — but he was friendly.

The little kiwi was starting to get a little less frightened of the dark
when he saw two pairs of eyes shining up ahead.
Then came a terrifying gurgling, coughing, rattling noise.
"What was that?" screamed Kiwi as he squeezed close to his mother's leg.

"Sorry," said a voice from the dark. A furry animal with a big tail —
and shining eyes — came loping out.
"This is possum," said Mother Kiwi.
"Hello," said a small voice from the possum's pouch.
"Mum was growling because she thought someone was going
to take some fruit from our tree."

"Th-that's okay," stammered the little kiwi. But it wasn't really okay.
He was still trembling from the fright he'd had.
"I'll make sure it's not you before I do it again next time," said the mother possum.
"Thank you," said the little kiwi. But he thought, there won't be a 'next time' —
not in the dark anyway! No. The night was too scary.
He'd go for his walks in the daytime from now on.

They got back to their burrow just before daybreak and nestled down to sleep through the day. The little kiwi was very tired after such a nerve-racking night. But he awoke early — when the sun was still shining — and thought, "This is a better time to go walking!"

Out he trotted, into the sunshine. It was a bit bright for his eyes, even in the bush, but at least the scary darkness had gone.

Down to the frog patch he scurried. But it was all silent.
He couldn't see or hear a frog anywhere.
Even the insects seemed to have gone. He felt a little lonely.

So he found the clump of ferns where the kakapo had been booming
and saw the little kakapo tucked up with his dad, fast asleep.
"Hello," the little kiwi whispered, just loud enough to wake him.
"Want to come and play?"
"Mmph, chomp, smack, mumble ..." the kakapo tried to say. "But it's still day-
time. I can't go out until dark." Then he rolled over and went back to sleep.

The little kiwi felt even more lonely.
He found the possum way up a tree, and the morepork too.

But they were sound asleep and didn't even move when
the little kiwi called out.

Poor Kiwi. He was very lonely.

In fact, the silent bush was suddenly even more scary than it was at night.

He hurried home and nestled in beside his mother again.
After their sleep, they'd go for another walk and see everyone again —
in the dark.

Perhaps the dark wasn't so bad after all.